CONTEN[TS]

D1349474

THE INTERPRETATION

Once Emperor Akbar was sitting in his court with a gloomy face. Many astrologers were also present there. When Birbal entered the court, he also found the emperor very sad.

Birbal asked the emperor, "What happened, Lord? Why do you seem so sad?"

"Birbal, yesterday I had a very bad dream. I saw that all my teeth had fallen off except one. I have called all these astrologers to interpret my dream," replied Akbar.

"And what do they say, Your Majesty?" asked Birbal.

"Ask them yourself," replied the emperor. Birbal turned to the astrologers and asked them what they thought about the dream.

"We consulted among ourselves and reached the

conclusion that this dream means that all the relatives of the emperor will die before him," replied the astrologers.

The emperor felt very upset and went to his royal chamber. Birbal followed him. He said to the emperor, "Your Majesty, I also have knowledge about astrology. According to me, the astrologers have misinterpreted your dream."

"Is that so?" asked Akbar with a little hope on his face. "Then what is the right interpretation of my dream?"

"Your Majesty, your dream means that you will live longer than your relatives," answered Birbal. Akbar's face lit up with a smile. Birbal had given the dream a new meaning by looking at it from a different point of view. Akbar rewarded Birbal with a bagful of gold coins.

THE ADVANCE PAYMENT

Once a horse trader came to the court of Emperor Akbar. He wanted to show the emperor some Arabian horses. Akbar was a great lover of good horses. After inspecting the horses, he liked them so much that he bought all of them and even paid advance money to the trader to get him more of such horses. The trader took the money and left the court. Months rolled by but he did not come back. He simply disappeared from the kingdom. Birbal felt very upset by this thoughtlessness on the emperor's part. Akbar completely forgot about the horse trader.

Some days later, the emperor asked Birbal to compile a list of all the fools in the kingdom. Birbal thus got an opportunity against the emperor's unmindful attitude. When Birbal presented the list,

Akbar read it carefully. Suddenly his face clouded with anger. He asked Birbal to be called immediately.

"Birbal," roared the emperor as soon as he saw him entering the chamber, "what is my name doing in this list?" The emperor sounded very angry.

"Well, Your Majesty, is it not true that you have been cheated by the horse trader?" asked Birbal.

"If the horse trader cheated me, does it mean that I am a fool?" asked Akbar.

"Was it not foolish to trust a stranger? You should have made inquiries about him," answered Birbal.

"When the trader returns…," the emperor began to say. "I will remove your name from this list," Birbal said completing the sentence. Akbar kept quiet as he had realised his mistake.

QUICK-WITTED BIRBAL

Akbar was in the habit of testing the intelligence of Birbal by asking him tricky questions. One day, he drew a line on the ground and asked Birbal, "Can you make this line smaller without rubbing it or cutting it?"

Birbal immediately bent down and drew a longer line. This made the first line look smaller.

"What is the thing that even the sun and the moon also cannot see?" the emperor fired another question.

"It is darkness Your Majesty," replied Birbal.

"What is the difference between the truth and lie?"the emperor asked again.

"It is the difference between seeing and hearing, Your Majesty. What one hears might be false but seeing is believing."

Akbar was satisfied with Birbal's answers and he gave him a necklace as a gift.

BANGLES AND STAIRS

One day, Akbar asked Birbal jovially, "Tell me Birbal, how many bangles does your wife wear? I'm sure you know the answer."

Birbal was unable to answer the question 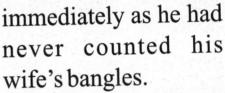 immediately as he had never counted his wife's bangles.

"What is this Birbal? You, who keeps track of so many things, do not know the number of bangles on your wife's hand?" For once, Birbal had been caught off guard and the emperor took full advantage of it.

Now Birbal himself was a quick-witted person and could not stay outwitted for long.

After two days, Birbal went to the king and asked, "Your Majesty,

do you know the number of soldiers in your army?"

"Of course," replied the emperor, "it is two lakhs."

"And do you know the number of stairs in your palace?"asked Birbal with a smile. The emperor was stupefied, for he had never counted the stairs in his palace. "No," came the reply from Akbar.

"Your Majesty, you climb up and down the stairs of your palace daily, still you do not know the number of stairs. Even though you know the number of soldiers in your army. Why is it so?" The emperor could not give any answer.

"We only remember important things. Since the number of bangles on my wife's hand is not important, I never counted them," said Birbal.

Akbar laughed heartily and praised Birbal.

THE PERSIAN LION

The king of Persia and Akbar had friendly relations between them. They often sent each other gifts and invitations. Sometimes, they also sent puzzles to each other to test the calibre of the courtiers of each other's court. One day, a messenger arrived at Emperor Akbar's court from the king of Persia with a gift. When the gift was brought to the court, everyone was stunned for a moment. It was a large cage with a lion in it. It was only after some time that they noticed that the lion was not moving, it was only a statue.

The Persian king had also sent a message along with it. He had asked that the cage should be returned safely and without breaking it after taking out the lion.

"Well, it is not a difficult task at all," said Akbar. "Open the gate and take out the lion," he ordered. But to their amazement the cage had no gate. Now everyone was puzzled. How to take out the lion without breaking the cage?

Some of the courtiers thought of breaking the lion into small pieces to take it out. But that was also not possible as the lion seemed to be made of some metal.

At last, the emperor summoned Birbal and said to him, "The king of Persia wants the lion to be taken out without breaking the cage. Can this be done?"

Birbal inspected the cage and the lion closely. After thinking for a while, an idea struck his mind. He scratched the surface of the lion, and found that the lion was made of wax. It was only given a showy

coating of metal to fool those who looked at it. "It can be done, Your Majesty, but it would take some time," said Birbal.

"Take all the time you need," said the emperor. "But solve this problem."

Next day, Birbal came to the court carrying some iron rods with wooden handles. He ordered the court servant to heat them up. Then he pushed the iron rods into the lion's statue.

The wax lion started melting on being heated. Soon all of it came out. Akbar felt very pleased with Birbal. He rewarded Birbal handsomely for his intelligence. Once again the Persian king was defeated.

One day, Akbar and Birbal were eating a dish of brinjal. Akbar started praising the dish very much.

"There is nothing tastier than this dish," said Akbar.

"You are right, Your Majesty," said Birbal. "It is indeed a tasty dish." Akbar called the servant and said, "Bring some more brinjal for Birbal."

"No, no," Birbal protested. "I don't like brinjal, please don't give me anymore." Akbar was greatly surprised.

"But just now you said that this dish is very tasty," said Akbar.

"Yes, Your Majesty, I am your servant and it is my duty to agree with you. But it does not mean that I would change my taste. I really don't like brinjal," replied Birbal. Akbar was surprised at this reply, but he accepted Birbal's explanation.

KEEP YOUR PROMISE

A poor man once came to Akbar's court. He pleaded that he was very poor and in dire need of help. The emperor promised to help him. But as the emperor had a lot of work, he forgot all about the poor man after a few days. One day, he was walking with Birbal when he saw a camel. "Tell me Birbal, why is the shape of a camel's neck so strange?" Akbar asked.

"Your Majesty, I have heard from a sage that anyone who forgets after making a promise is punished in this way by God. It is possible that the camel had broken a promise," replied Birbal. The emperor started thinking about Birbal's reply. Suddenly, he remembered the promise that he had made to the poor man.

He understood what Birbal was trying to say. The very next day, Akbar called that poor man and gave him enough money to lead his life happily. In this way, Birbal often helped the needy.

UNDERSTANDING ONE'S MIND

One day Akbar was sitting and looking at himself in the mirror. Suddenly he seemed to have noticed something. He immediately called a servant and said, "Go and call him."

The servant quickly went out. On the way, he remembered that he had forgotten to ask whom to call. The servant was in a dilemma. He did not want to go back as the emperor would get angry at him for not asking earlier. He went about asking the other servants what the emperor might have meant, but no one had any reply.

At last, one of the servants told him, "You should go to Birbal, only he knows the mind of the emperor."

So the servant went to Birbal's house. After he had narrated the entire incident, Birbal thought for a while. Then he asked, "What was the emperor doing when he sent for you?"

"He was looking at himself in the mirror," replied the servant.

"Very well, then go and get a

barber," said Birbal.

Birbal had understood that the hair or beard of the emperor had grown. 'Doubtless he had noticed it while looking at the mirror and wanted a hair cut or a shave,' Birbal reasoned to himself.

In the palace, the emperor remembered after the servant had gone that he had not told him whom to call. He was going out to send another servant after him when he saw the servant returning with the barber. He was very surprised.

"How did you know that I wanted a barber?" he asked.

"I did not know that, Your Majesty. It was Birbal that helped me out," replied the servant. The emperor could not but admire Birbal's intelligence.

DONKEYS DON'T EAT TOBACCO

Birbal was in the habit of chewing tobacco. Akbar had warned him against this habit many a times, but Birbal had got addicted to it. One day, the emperor was passing through a field with Birbal. Nearby, there was a tobacco field. Just then they saw a donkey approaching the tobacco field. But as soon as the donkey came near the field it turned away in disgust. The emperor said, "Look Birbal, even a donkey does not want to eat tobacco."

"Yes, Your Majesty, a donkey does not have enough sense to appreciate tobacco," replied Birbal.

Akbar was once again left speechless by Birbal's wit. But after pausing for a while, he said, "Birbal, I appreciate your wit, but chewing of tobacco is

injurious to health and you also know this. You should stop chewing tobacco."

Birbal knew that the emperor was right. "I would try to give up this habit, Your Majesty," he said.

THE UNLUCKY

There was a courtier in the court of Akbar named Radhumal. He was a very superstitious man. One day, he started telling the emperor that a certain person by the name of Manohar was very unlucky. Whoever saw his face in the morning had a bad day.

"Lord, the whole kingdom is aware of this fact. I can present many persons in front of you who suffered badly just because they had seen Manohar's face in the morning," Radhumal informed Akbar.

"What nonsense!" said the emperor, "Such a thing is not possible. Tomorrow I would call him in the morning and prove you wrong." The emperor ordered his servant to go and inform Manohar that he should come early morning the next day. The emperor and Manohar met in the royal garden the next day. As they were talking Akbar got the news that one of his granaries had caught fire. Akbar immediately sent some men to assess the damage. After some time as the emperor was going back to the palace, he slipped and fell down the stairs and got hurt. 'What is happening today?' he wondered. After having lunch when he came back, he again met Radhumal.

"Your Majesty, did not I tell you that Manohar was very unlucky! You should send him away immediately," said Radhumal.

The emperor had also become afraid. He decided to imprison Manohar. He called his guards and asked them to put Manohar behind bars.

The guards immediately went to Manohar's place and arrested the poor man. All of his pleas that he was innocent fell on deaf ears. As Manohar was being taken away, he met Birbal. "What happened, Manohar?" Birbal asked in surprise. Manohar

tearfully narrated the entire incident.

"Is that all? Do as I say and you would be released," said Birbal and whispered something in his ear. After some time the guards brought Manohar back to the emperor for the trial.

When the trial began in the court, Manohar defended himself, "Your Majesty, you are imprisoning me because you think that I am unlucky. But after seeing your face I am being imprisoned. Tell me who is more unlucky?" he asked the emperor. Akbar could not help smiling at this.

"I would let you go but tell me, was it Birbal who gave you this idea?"

Manohar nodded in affirmation. The king realised that all which happened to him was just his fate and Manohar was not responsible. He ordered Manohar to be released.

AKBAR'S RING

One day, Akbar was strolling with Birbal in the city. As they passed by a field they saw an old well there. "Let us see what is in it," said Akbar. They peeped into the well. It was a very deep well but had gone dry.

"It seems that this well is lying useless from years," said the emperor. "I don't think anything can be taken out from it."

"It is possible, but it would take some time," said Birbal. At this, the emperor took out his ring and threw it into the well. "Let me see if you can take it out," challenged the emperor. As they were going back, Birbal took a lump of cow dung, and unnoticed by the emperor, threw it into the well. Some weeks later they both were strolling near the same well.

Akbar was surprised to see it brimming with water.

"Who filled this well with water?" asked the emperor. He also saw that a lump of cow dung was floating in water. "I did it Your Majesty," replied Birbal and picked up the lump of cow dung and turned it over. On its other side, the emperor's ring was embedded.

"How did this happen?" asked the emperor in surprise.

"I had thrown cow dung on the ring that day. As the cow dung dried up, the ring got stuck in it. When I made the well filled with water, it came up to the brim as it is lighter in weight than water," replied Birbal. The emperor was so pleased that he gifted the ring to Birbal.

THE GUILTY THIEF

One day, a burglary took place in a merchant's mansion. The merchant thought that it must be a misdeed of one of his servants. He asked all his servants about it but no one admitted the theft.

The merchant then went to Birbal, his friend and told him the entire matter. Birbal deliberated for some time. He thought of a plan. He went to the merchant's mansion with him and called all the servants. When the servants assembled before him, Birbal asked them, "You all must be aware of the theft that took place in your master's mansion yesterday night. He thinks that one of you has committed the crime. The one who is guilty come forward."

But none of the servants came forward. Then Birbal gave each of them a stick and declared, "These sticks are no ordinary. They

have magical powers. All the sticks are of equal length. The stick of the guilty will grow two inches by tomorrow morning. Now you all can go home."

While everybody slept peacefully, the servant who had done the theft was thinking about the stick. Next morning, he cut his stick by two inches.

Later in the day, all the servants showed their sticks to Birbal. Birbal examined the sticks and found one of the sticks shorter than the other ones. He pulled the servant out of the queue and said to the merchant, "Friend, here is your thief."

The servant fell at the merchant's feet and asked for forgiveness. The merchant thanked Birbal and asked him how he came to know about the culprit.

Birbal told him the entire plan on which he had worked. The merchant was impressed by Birbal's cleverness.

A TRIP TO HEAVEN

The personal barber of Akbar was very jealous of Birbal. He was looking for the opportunity to harm Birbal. One day he thought of a plan. As he was shaving the emperor, he started talking, "Your Majesty, do you believe in next life?"

"Yes, I do," replied Akbar. "Well then, do you have a wish to find out how your relatives are living in heaven?" the barber asked.

"Yes, I do want to find out, but how is it possible? No one can go to heaven," replied the emperor.

"There are some saints who can send a person to heaven. I will make all the arrangements. You will just have to choose a person who can go ," said the barber.

"That is very easy," said the emperor. "I will send Birbal. But how is such a thing going to happen?"

"That is easy. A pyre would be lit and Birbal would be made to sit on it. As the flames of the pyre would rise, he would also rise with them. Finally, he would be transported to heaven," said the barber.

When the emperor mentioned this plan to Birbal, he at once understood that someone had plotted against him. "Who made this wonderful plan?" he asked.

"It is my barber," said the emperor.

"I am quite ready to go to heaven, Your Majesty, but I need some time for the preparation," said Birbal.

The emperor gave him time. Later, Birbal found out the exact location where the pyre was placed, and had a tunnel dug from beneath it to his house. After the preparations were complete, he gave the go ahead to be taken to the cremation ground. Once the pyre was lit Birbal escaped, through the tunnel, to his house. The Barber was very happy as he thought his enemy was dead. After spending a few months in his house, Birbal came to the court. During the days

of secret living, Birbal appeared before Akbar with beard. The emperor was overjoyed to see him. "Welcome Birbal," the emperor said. "How is everything in heaven? How are my relatives?"

"Lord, everything is fine in heaven and your father and grandfather have sent you their regards. But there is only one problem. There is no barber in heaven. You can see that even I have not been able to have a haircut or shave there. They have asked you to send them a good barber," replied Birbal.

"Yes, yes, I will certainly fulfil their wish," the emperor said happily. "I'll send my own barber to them." Saying so, the emperor asked his barber to prepare. The Barber protested a lot but it was set aside, and one day he was burnt on the pyre. In this way, Birbal revenged on the wicked barber.

THE MANGO KERNELS

Once Akbar and Birbal were both sitting and relishing mangoes. Birbal was regaling Akbar with anecdotes and stories. Akbar was enjoying himself immensely. After eating the mangoes, they were both throwing the mango kernels below the table. Suddenly, Akbar thought of a plan. He slowly pushed his pile of kernels to Birbal's side. Then he said loudly, "Birbal, I did not know that you could eat so many mangoes. Are you this greedy for mangoes?"

When Birbal looked down he was surprised to see so many mango kernels. Then he looked below Akbar's seat and saw there was not even a single kernel. He immediately understood what Akbar had done.

"I am very fond of mangoes, Your Majesty, but you are much more fond of them. I have eaten only the mangoes while you have eaten their kernels as well," said Birbal. Akbar praised quick-witted Birbal.

THE SCHOLAR OF LANGUAGES

One day, a learned but proud scholar came to the court of Akbar. He claimed that he knew all the languages of the world and can converse in any language fluently.

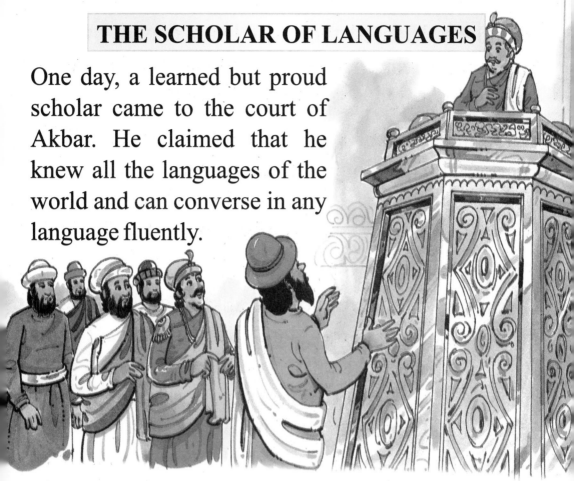

The scholar said to the emperor, "Sir, I want every courtier to question me in their own mother tongue and I will answer them in that language only." Many courtiers asked him questions in their mother tongue and the scholar gave the answer to each person's question fluently in their respective languages.

The emperor and the courtiers were greatly impressed by him. The scholar then challenged the emperor, "Sir, I challenge all of your courtiers to guess my mother tongue until tomorrow morning. If anyone could tell my mother tongue then I will salute him and quietly go away from here. Otherwise I should be declared the most learned man in your kingdom." Akbar agreed and ordered his servants to arrange for a night's stay for the scholar.

When the scholar left the court, Akbar asked all his courtiers if they could tell the mother tongue of the scholar. None came forward. Then Akbar looked at Birbal and said, "Birbal, our honour is at stake. Only you can help us."

Birbal said that he would give answer of the question the next morning in the court. Then Birbal went to the room in which the scholar was asleep. He took a piece of hay and tickled the scholar's ears. The scholar felt irritated and changed his side. Birbal continued with the tickling.

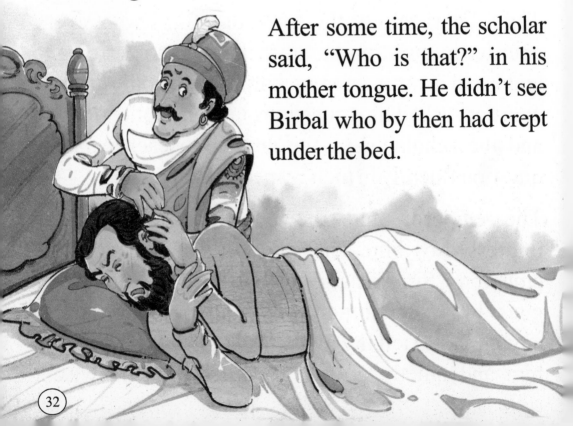

After some time, the scholar said, "Who is that?" in his mother tongue. He didn't see Birbal who by then had crept under the bed.

Next morning, the scholar went to the court and took his seat. Akbar looked at Birbal. At first, Birbal counted him many languages to which the scholar nodded in the negative and felt more proud. At last, Birbal said politely to the scholar, "Sir, is your mother tongue Telugu?"

The scholar nodded his head in the affirmative. He was surprised how Birbal came to know about his mother tongue. He accepted that Birbal was the most learned person in the kingdom. The emperor gave so many gifts to the scholar and bade him goodbye. When the scholar left the court, the emperor asked Birbal how he came to know about the scholar's mother tongue.

Birbal said, "Your Majesty, even though a man can speak so many languages but at the time of difficulty, he only speaks in his own language." Then he narrated how he managed to know the answer. The emperor burst into laughter.

One day a brahmin came to meet Akbar to seek his help. He was in need of some money. Now there were some courtiers in Akbar's court who liked to have fun at somebody else's expense. One of such courtiers stood up and said to the brahmin, "Can you stand in the cold waters of the Yamuna for the whole night? If you succeed, Emperor Akbar will reward you." The emperor also agreed to this.

That night, the brahmin stood in the cold waters of the Yamuna the whole night. Emperor Akbar had appointed a guard to keep an eye on the brahmin. Next morning, the guard reached the court with the brahmin. He assured the emperor that the brahmin had stood the whole night in the cold water. "How were you able to spend the entire night in the cold water?" the emperor asked in an amazed voice.

"I got solace from watching the lamps of your palace, Your Majesty," the brahmin replied politely.

At this, the emperor said, "Then I will not give you any reward. You were able to stand in the cold water as you were getting warmth from the lamps."

The brahmin felt very sad and went away. Birbal was also present there. He felt very angry with the emperor at this injustice. He decided to do something to help the poor brahmin.

The next day Birbal did not appear in the court. Akbar ordered a man to go and see why Birbal had not come. The man returned and said that Birbal was cooking *khichdi* and would come after eating it. A long time passed by and still, Birbal did not come to the palace.

Emperor Akbar again sent a man to see what was delaying him, and again he got the same information. At last, he himself went to see which type of *khichdi* Birbal was cooking that was taking so much time.

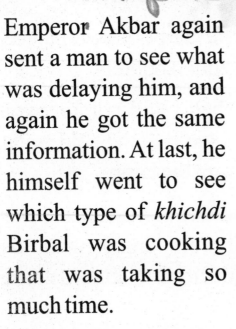

When he reached Birbal's place, Akbar found that he had hung the pot of *khichdi* on a high branch of a tree, and below it, he had lighted a small fire.

"Birbal, what is this?" asked the emperor. "Is it possible for the heat of the fire to reach the pot from such a distance? Your

khichdi would never get cooked in this way."

"Why, Lord? If that brahmin could receive the warmth from the lamps of the palace, which were so far away then why can't the warmth of the fire reach this pot which is much nearer?" replied Birbal.

Emperor Akbar at once realised his mistake. He also understood Birbal's purpose for cooking his *khichdi* in an extraordinary way. "Birbal, I understand your meaning. That brahmin would get his reward. Now can you hurry up with your *khichdi* ? I need your attendance at the court."

Birbal left his *khichdi* and gladly went with the emperor. Next day, the brahmin was called at the court and was rewarded by the emperor.

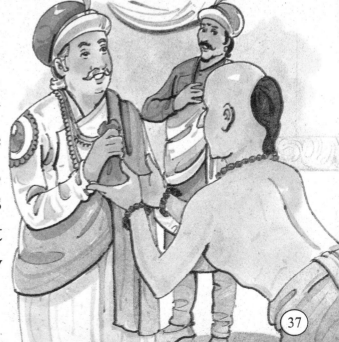

THE NUMBER OF SPARROWS

One day, a messenger visited Emperor Akbar's court. He had come from the neighbouring kingdom. The king of that kingdom had heard a lot about the wit and intelligence of Birbal. Therefore, he had sent his messenger to test the wit of Birbal. After giving presents, he said "Your Majesty, my king has heard a lot about the intelligence of your famous courtier, Birbal. Therefore, he has sent me with a question for him."

"What is your question?" asked Birbal.

"Can you tell me how many sparrows are there in Agra?" asked the messenger. Everyone became worried on hearing this question. They were wondering how Birbal would answer such a question. But Birbal replied without the slightest hesitation, "I

know the answer. It is 88,457."

The messenger was surprised. He thought that Birbal was trying to fool him. "What if the number is more than that?" he asked.

"Well then it means some of the relatives of the sparrows from other cities are visiting them," Birbal replied calmly.

"And what if the number is less than that?" again asked the messenger.

"It means some of the sparrows of Agra have gone to visit their relatives in other cities," Birbal again replied with a smile. "If you do not believe me, you can any time count yourself and know the fact."

Everyone started laughing. The messenger praised the intelligence of Birbal and returned to his kingdom.

MEN OR HENS

One day, Emperor Akbar decided to make fun of Birbal. Before Birbal came to court, the emperor gave one egg each to all his courtiers which they were instructed to hide in their clothes. Then he gave them some instructions. When Birbal arrived, the emperor said, "I saw in my dream yesterday that a miracle is going to take place. Those of my courtiers who are loyal to me would be able to produce an egg today. Therefore, I want all of you to produce an egg." Everyone quickly produced eggs from within their clothes. Birbal was very surprised. He immediately understood that the emperor was trying to make fun of him. He said, "Your Majesty, I am sorry to say that I would not be able to produce an egg. Because only hens can produce eggs, and I am a man, not a hen." All the courtiers who were standing there holding their eggs went red with embarrassment. The emperor started laughing at Birbal's wit.

THE SHADOWY PLAY

One day, Emperor Akbar got annoyed with Birbal and asked him to leave the kingdom. Birbal being a person of self-respect said to the emperor, "OK, Your Majesty, I am leaving this kingdom right now. I will not return until you ask me to."

Birbal left the kingdom with his family. After some days, Akbar started missing Birbal. He asked his men to search for Birbal in all the neighbouring kingdoms but to no avail. He was nowhere to be found.

Emperor Akbar thought of a plan. He proclaimed a reward of a thousand gold coins for the man who would enter his court in half light and half shadow. Akbar knew that only Birbal would be able to solve the puzzle.

Meanwhile, Birbal was staying with a brahmin's family in a distant kingdom. When he came to know about the proclamation, he could not resist himself

41

from solving the puzzle. Birbal asked the brahmin to go to Emperor Akbar's court and solve the puzzle. The brahmin said to Birbal, "I didn't even understand the puzzle and you are asking me to solve it." Birbal advised him to take a cot over his head and enter the court of Emperor Akbar. In this way he would be in half light and half shadow.

The next day, the brahmin entered Akbar's court with a cot over his head. Akbar said to him, "You have solved the puzzle. Now tell me, did you think of this solution yourself or someone else told you about this?" The brahmin told Akbar that a guest of his had told him the solution of the puzzle. Akbar understand that guest was Birbal. He immediately sent his men to fetch Birbal. Akbar was happy having Birbal again by his side.

COUNTING THE UNCOUNTABLE

One night as Akbar was standing on his terrace with Birbal, he looked up and saw the stars littering the sky. "Birbal, can you tell me the exact number of the stars in the sky?" asked Akbar.

"Yes, Your Majesty," replied Birbal. "As many as the hair on a horse's head."

"But Birbal," Akbar said after thinking for sometime, "the hair on the head of a horse are uncountable."

"Yes, Your Majesty, so are the stars."

The emperor was struck speechless by this reply.

HOW MANY TURNS?

One day, a messenger came to the court of Akbar and said, "The Afghan king has send his greetings. He has expressed his wish to come and visit Agra. But he wants to know beforehand how many turns the streets of Agra have, so that he may not get confused when he comes here."

Emperor Akbar replied, "It would take some time to find out exactly how many turns the streets of Agra have. I would send a reply after a month."

"No, Your Majesty," the messenger said, "the king told me to bring the answer with me, and I have to leave by tomorrow."

Now Emperor Akbar was really in a fix. He was still debating what should be done when Birbal came in the court. Emperor Akbar was relieved to see him.

"I have received a strange request, Birbal," said the Emperor. "The king of Afghanistan wants to know how many turns our streets have, and I have to give the reply by tomorrow."

"It is a very easy question, Your Majesty. The king of Afghanistan should know the answer," replied Birbal.

"Do you know the answer?" asked Akbar excitedly.

"Yes, Your Majesty. All the streets in the world have only two turns, a left turn and a right turn." The emperor was very pleased with Birbal's reply.

"You have once again saved the prestige of the kingdom with your wit," said Akbar and praised Birbal.

THE ALCHEMIST'S STONE

One day, one of the ambassadors at the court of Akbar asked him, "Great king, in our country there are many great alchemists who have a special stone that can turn an ordinary metal into gold. It is also used to differentiate between gold and brass. Do you have something similar in your kingdom?"

"Yes," said the emperor. "I have a gem that can do something even better. It can not only distinguish between gold and brass, it can also distinguish between all the good and the bad things."

"Such a thing should really be a miracle," said the ambassador. "Can you show it to me?"

"Yes," said Akbar and called Birbal. "Here is my touchstone, he can distinguish between good and bad things."

"Oh, we have also heard about him. You are really lucky to have Birbal," said the ambassador.

LOAD OF THREE DONKEYS

One day, Emperor Akbar decided to take a bath in the river. He went there with Birbal and his two sons.

Before entering into the river water, Akbar and his sons gave

their clothes to Birbal who decided to wait for them on the river side.

While Akbar was taking bath, he felt like teasing Birbal. He gave a smile to Birbal and said, "Birbal, you seem like a donkey carrying a pile of clothes."

Birbal at once retorted, "Yes, Your Majesty, but there is a difference. In this case, I am not carrying the load of one donkey, but of three."

This statement left the emperor speechless. Birbal had again given a proof of his witty nature. Akbar praised the sense of humour of Birbal.

THE REASON OF GETTING FAT

One day, Birbal teased Akbar for being fat. "It is because of the rich diet I am fed by the cook," retorted Akbar.

"No, Your Majesty, it is because you are without any tension. A person who has worries would not get fat even if he is fed with rich diets," said Birbal.

"I don't agree with you. Even if an animal is fed well, it becomes fat," said the emperor. "Now, you would have to prove your point."

Next day, Birbal bought a goat from the market and took it to his house. He asked his servants to feed it very well. A month passed by. One day, Akbar went to inspect the goat.

He was surprised to find that the goat had not gained any weight. "Birbal, I am surprised. Did you really feed it well?"

"Your Majesty, you can enquire yourself from the servants," said Birbal.

"Then why it has not gained weight?" asked Akbar.

"I had got it tied to the cage of a lion, therefore, though it was fed a nice meal twice a day, it did not gain weight. You see, tension in us as well as in animals keep us away from gaining weight."

The emperor conceded that Birbal had proved his point.

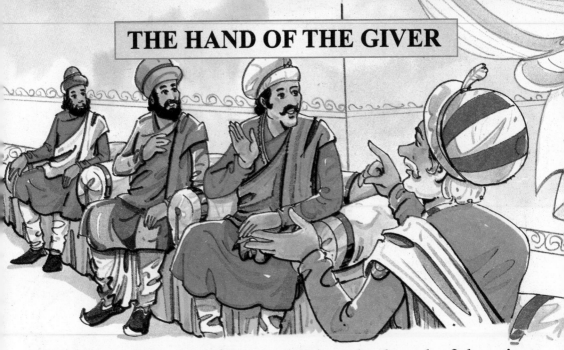

One day, emperor Akbar said that the hand of the giver is always above the hand of the receiver. The courtiers agreed. Then the emperor looked at Birbal.

"Well Birbal, what is your opinion?"

"I think it may not always be so, Your Majesty," replied Birbal.

"Well then tell me when is the hand of the giver below the hand of the receiver?" asked Akbar irritatingly. 'Birbal argues even when everything is clear,' thought Akbar.

"The hand of the giver is below that of the receiver when he is offering snuff," replied Birbal.

Akbar could not but admire Birbal's powers of observation. He understood that he had got irritated at Birbal needlessly.

THE STRANGE REWARD

One day, Birbal came to know that the guards of the palace had become corrupt. Birbal started thinking of ways to verify this news. Finally he decided to go to the palace in disguise. He went there in the disguise of a Persian poet. On reaching the gate, he said to the guards in a whining voice, "Please let me go to the court. I want to meet the emperor."

"You cannot go in," said one guard in a stern voice.

On being asked the reason, the guard replied, "The emperor is very busy."

"But I am no ordinary person. I am a poet I have come to India to recite my poems to the emperor," Birbal again pleaded.

"You can go in but you will have to give half of your reward to us," said the guard. Birbal agreed.

"But remember that the emperor should not be told anything about it in the court. He already knows about it. It is the custom in this kingdom," cautioned the guard.

Birbal agreed to him. He went

to the court and recited
many poems. Emperor
Akbar felt very pleased and said to disguised Birbal,
"I want to reward you for it. What do you want?"

"I want 100 lashes," replied Birbal. Everyone was
shocked. "Why do you want such a thing?" asked
Akbar. "Your Majesty, I have to distribute it among
other people, therefore, I do not mind," Birbal
replied. The emperor was even more surprised. "Who
do you have to share the reward with?"

"With the guards," said Birbal and narrated to Akbar
the entire episode with the guards. The emperor was
very angry. He immediately asked the guards to be
whipped.

"I would like you to stay in my court," said the emperor.

"I am already in your court, Your Majesty," said
Birbal and removed his disguise.

THE MARRIAGE OF SEA

Once Akbar became angry with Birbal for some reason. He asked Birbal to leave his court. Birbal went away quietly. Some days passed and Akbar started missing Birbal. He sent out a search party for him, but to no avail.

Akbar knew that Birbal could never resist challenges. He decided to announce a question that only Birbal would be able to answer. Next day, he sent out a proposal to all the neighbouring kings that he wanted to get the sea of his kingdom married, so they should send the rivers of their kingdoms to him.

No one answered for some time then a reply came

from one of the kings. It read, 'We are ready to send our rivers for the marriage but ask the wells of your kingdom to come half way to receive them.' Akbar at once understood that this reply could have only been sent by Birbal, so he sent his envoy to bring him back.

THE MOST BEAUTIFUL CHILD

Akbar had a grandson whom he loved very much. One day, he started praising him in the court. "My grandson is the most beautiful child in the whole world," said the emperor. No one said anything.

Birbal was also present in the court. He got up and said, "You think so because you are the grandfather of the child." The emperor got very angry at this.

"Very well then," said the emperor, "go and find me a more beautiful child."

The very next day Birbal took Akbar to a remote part of the city. There they saw a child playing in the dirt.

"Your Majesty, this is the most beautiful child in the world," said Birbal. The emperor took a look at the child. He was dark complexioned, and a part of his

face had a big white patch. "You call this child beautiful?" asked Akbar. "He is the ugliest child that I have ever seen."

As soon as he said this, a woman came running out of a nearby hut and started berating Akbar, "How dare you call my child ugly? He is the most beautiful child in the world. You people have no idea about children. Just go away from here."

Then the woman took the child and went inside the hut, kissing him all the while.

"You were right, Birbal. Everyone thinks that his or her child is the most beautiful in the whole world," said the emperor. Birbal didn't say anything. He just smiled softly.

ALIVE OR DEAD

During the time of Emperor Akbar, there were nine talented people in his court. They were called the nine gems. Birbal was one of them. He was an extremely intelligent and witty man. He often helped people who were in trouble. Because of these qualities, he was loved by all and sundry.

Once the manservant of Emperor Akbar came running to Birbal. He was perspiring and looked very worried. His name was Sitaram. "What is the matter, Sitaram?" Birbal asked. "Some days ago, the emperor had given me a parrot for safekeeping. It had been given to the emperor by a holy fakir. The emperor had told me that I must look after the bird well, and nothing untoward should happen to the parrot. He had said that whoever brought the news of the parrot's death to him, would be hanged."

"So, what is wrong now?" asked Birbal.

"The parrot has died. In spite of all my care, it is now lying dead in its cage."

"Are you sure, it is not just taking a little nap?" asked Birbal.

"No sir, I am sure the parrot is dead. Please tell me some way to face the emperor," said the manservant.

"Don't worry and go back home. I will inform the emperor of the parrot's death and run the risk of getting hanged," assured Birbal.

Sitaram thanked him and went back. Later in the day, Birbal went to Akbar's court and said to him, "Your Majesty, I just visited the parrot given to you by the holy fakir. It is truly a holy parrot. I found it immersed in deep thought, lying on its side."

The emperor was really surprised to hear this. He said, "If what you say is true, it is really a thing to wonder at. I would go and see it with my courtiers." As soon as the emperor saw the parrot, he knew that the parrot was dead. "Birbal, anyone can see that the parrot is dead, and don't tell me that you did not know it."

"Yes, Your Majesty, but I did not want to be hanged, therefore, I had to take recourse to this method. Everything that is born dies, and you must not punish Sitaram for the death of the parrot," said Birbal. The emperor understood Birbal's reason for lying. He smiled and said, "I forgive Sitaram, and I would give you some suitable reward for it."

Thus, Birbal was able to save a life by his intelligence.

CHILD, THE FATHER OF MAN

One day, Birbal arrived late in the court. Akbar was irked by this delay. As soon as Birbal arrived, Akbar asked him, "Birbal, you have come late again. May I know what is your excuse this time?"

Birbal was always ready with an answer, but this time he was a little hesitant to give his reply. "Your Majesty, actually…well as I was about to leave the house, my son started crying. How could I leave him crying?"

Everyone started laughing and whispering among themselves. "The great wit, Birbal was held up by a mere child," said one of the courtiers making fun of Birbal. Akbar too smiled and said, "I used to think that you were a very clever man. But it is quite clear now that I was mistaken. Where was your mind when your son was crying?"

"Your Majesty, fulfilling a child's wish is no child's play," Birbal replied.

"Nonsense!" the emperor said. "You just don't know how to handle a child. Bring him to me tomorrow, and I will show you how simple it is."

Next day, Birbal brought his four-year old child to the court. The emperor called the child nearer to the throne and picked him up in his lap.

"Well son, I am the emperor, and I can fulfill all your wishes. What would you like to have?" the emperor asked very sweetly. The boy did not listen to him. He jumped up and snatched away Akbar's crown, and threw it on the ground.

"I want a sugarcane," cried the child. Akbar immediately ordered

sugarcane to be brought. It was brought on a platter cut and peeled.

"No, I want a whole sugarcane," again shouted the child.

"Get a whole sugarcane," Akbar instructed his servants. A whole, unpeeled sugarcane was immediately brought in the court.

"No, make the same sugarcane whole again," the child said stubbornly. Akbar was stumped. He did not know what to do.

The courtiers had also started sniggering at Akbar's discomfiture. Akbar said to Birbal, "Birbal, take your child back home. He is too much for me. I cannot handle him."

Birbal smiled and said, "As you wish, Your Majesty." Akbar had realised that taking care of a child was no easy matter.

THE PUNISHMENT

One day, Akbar was taking a stroll in his royal palace. He soon reached an old part of the palace. There he saw that the plaster had peeled off from one section of the wall. He immediately called his servant.

"That wall looks like a blot on the beauty of my palace. Get it repaired immediately," Akbar ordered. The servant whose name was Dholak said, "Yes," and went away. Next day, the emperor again went that way to have a look. He wanted to see how the wall looked after being repaired. He was very offended when he saw the wall in the same state. He immediately called Dholak. "What is this?" he thundered. "Why have you not repaired the wall as yet?"

"I… I did not get enough time, Your Majesty," Dholak stammered.

"Didn't get enough time!" the emperor said angrily. "I will teach you a lesson for disobeying me. Go and get two bowls of lime." On the way, Dholak met

Birbal. Birbal immediately felt that something was wrong. "Dholak, why are you so worried?" asked Birbal. Dholak sobbed and told him the entire story. "Oh, don't worry. The emperor would ask you to eat lime as a punishment. I will give you something. Keep it in the other bowl. When the emperor asks you to eat, eat from the other bowl," advised Birbal.

When the emperor asked Dholak to eat the lime, Dholak started eating from the bowl in which the stuff that Birbal had prescribed was kept. Soon the emperor took pity on him and said, "That's enough."

'Poor Dholak,' thought the emperor. He would be sick for some days because of eating so much lime. But the next day, Akbar saw Dholak working as usual. He was very surprised. 'It seems that my punishment

did not have any effect,' the emperor thought and again called Dholak. He again asked him to bring two bowls of lime. As Dholak was going, he again met Birbal, and told him everything. Birbal understood that this time the emperor would want him to eat both the bowls of lime. So he instructed Dholak to take the stuff he had prescribed him earlier in both the bowls. Dholak did as instructed. Sure enough, the emperor this time asked Dholak to eat the lime of both the bowls. He started watching carefully to see if Dholak shows any sign of illness. But Dholak merrily went on eating lime. The emperor became suspicious. "Show me the bowls," he asked Dholak. He inspected the bowls carefully. When he tasted the lime, he found that actually it was white butter. "Who gave you this idea?" Akbar asked Dholak. "If you tell me the truth, I will let you go." Dholak said with fright, "Your Majesty, it was the idea of Birbal."

The emperor laughed and let him go.

THE EXACT PAINTING

The royal painter at Akbar's court had a problem. He did not know how to solve it. After much thought, he decided that he should consult Birbal regarding the problem. He went to see Birbal.

"Come, Fazlji, what made you come this way today?"asked Birbal when he saw the painter. "Birbal, I have a problem," said the great painter.

"How can I help you?" Birbal said with a smile.

"Liaqat Ali, the rogue had commissioned me to paint a picture of him. He said that the picture must be exactly like him. I agreed. Last week, I went to his house and spent the entire day in painting his picture. That day he had a beard and a moustache. By nightfall I had completed the sketch. I said I would complete the painting and bring it after some time. Next day, when I went back with the complete painting, he had shaved off his beard. He refused to accept the painting on the ground that it was not his exact image. That day I

again spent the entire day painting his sketch. But when I took back the picture he had shaved off his moustache. In this way he has been troubling me everyday. I don't know what to do," said the painter.

"I see. I have an idea. Follow my advice closely and your problem would be solved," replied Birbal.

The next day, the painter went back to Liaqat Ali. "Well Fazlji, have you bring my picture?" asked Ali.

"Yes," the painter said and gave him a package wrapped in paper. As soon as Liaqat Ali opened the package, he found a mirror in it. He became angry, "I had asked for a painting and you are giving me a mirror."

"Yes, but you insisted that the picture should be exactly like you. Only a mirror can fulfil your wish. Keep this mirror," replied the painter. Liaqat Ali realised his mistake, and agreed to pay him the money for the pictures that he had painted. The painter returned and thanked Birbal profusely.

One day, the messenger of the king of Sri Lanka visited the palace of Emperor Akbar. He greeted the emperor and said, "Your Majesty, the king of Sri Lanka has come to know that there are many courtiers in your court who are full of intelligence. He has send me to get a pot full of intelligence from here."

Emperor Akbar looked at his courtiers who were murmuring among themselves and said, "The Sri Lankan king wants to make a fool of us. How can we provide him with a pot full of intelligence? It's weird!" Just then Birbal stood up and addressed the emperor, "I can arrange a pot full of intelligence for the Sri Lankan king but it will take a week's time."

The messenger had no problem in giving the time to Birbal as he was thinking that it was impossible to get a pot full of intelligence.

Birbal went to his home and said to his servant, "Go and get some small-mouthed earthen pots." The servant went to the market and soon returned with a dozen of earthen pots. Taking those earthen pots Birbal went to his garden where many pumpkins had been planted. He then placed the plants inside the pots. Then he asked his servant not to remove the pots till instructed.

After a week, Birbal went to the garden to check the pumpkin plants. He saw that the pumpkins had fully grown inside the pots. He asked his servant to remove the pots full of pumpkins carefully.

Next morning, Birbal went to the court and called upon the Sri Lankan messenger.

Giving him a pot whose mouth was covered with cloth, he said, "Sir, I present you a pot full of intelligence."

"Because intelligence is such a valuable asset, we keep them buried under the ground in earthen pots. I request you to empty the pot very carefully so that not even a scratch come on it. The fruit of intelligence will be effective only if it is removed without any tampering," continued Birbal.

The messenger of the king of Sri Lanka removed the cloth from the pot. He was taken aback to see a pumpkin in the earthen pot. He left the court without uttering even a single word.

When Emperor Akbar wanted to know what was inside the pot, Birbal sent for another pot from his house. Soon his servant returned with one. Akbar peeped inside the pot and was surprised to see a pumpkin. He said laughingly, "The Sri Lankan king would never wish for a pot of intelligence."

GOD'S LOVE

Emperor Akbar was always curious to learn more about different religions. He once asked Birbal a strange question, "Tell me Birbal, why did Lord Krishna run to help his devotees himself? Did he not have any servant?"

Birbal was surprised to hear this question. The emperor was a devout person and never criticised Gods. Akbar continued. "Not only this, all Gods behave rather strangely. They come whenever a devotee calls them. Should a God be at the beck and call of devotees?"

Birbal did not answer immediately. He said, "This is a point that cannot be explained like this. I would answer it later."

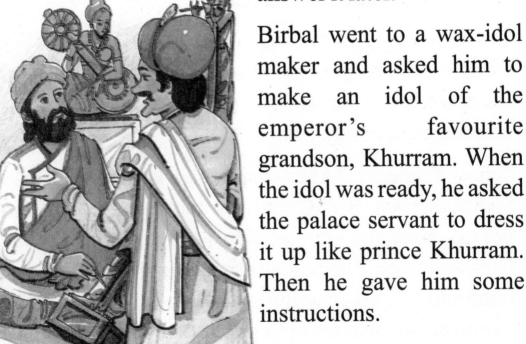

Birbal went to a wax-idol maker and asked him to make an idol of the emperor's favourite grandson, Khurram. When the idol was ready, he asked the palace servant to dress it up like prince Khurram. Then he gave him some instructions.

Next day, Birbal and the emperor were strolling in the garden. As soon as they came in sight of the lake, Birbal signalled to the servant. The servant who was carrying the idol threw it into the lake. From far it looked as if the prince had fallen in. Without waiting for a moment, Akbar rushed forward and jumped into the lake. When he reached the fake Khurram, he found that it was only a wax-idol. As Birbal helped him out of the water, he asked him, "Your Majesty, you have so many servants. What was the need to jump in yourself?"

"Birbal, Khurram is my dearest grandson. Should I have waited for my servants to save my grandson?" said the emperor.

"God also does not wait for others to help his devotees because he loves his devotees very much," said Birbal. Now Akbar understood that all this was Birbal's doing. He understood what Birbal wanted to make him understand.

THE TRICKSTER

Once, there lived a sage who was thought to be a very pious person. But, he was actually very greedy. Once, an old woman came to him. She said, "O pious sage, I am going on a pilgrimage. I have some copper coins that I have saved up over a lifetime. I have no one to leave them with. Would you kindly keep them in your possession?"

"My good woman, I do not like worldly things as I am quite above them. Keep the coins in the corner of the hut, or better bury them," the sage said and closed his eyes in meditation. The woman went and buried the coins in a corner of the hut.

Months rolled by, and the woman returned from her pilgrimage. She went to visit the sage. "O revered one, I have come back. May I have my coins so that I can live my life in peace?" the woman asked the sage.

"Go and get the coins from where you had buried them," said the sage. The woman went and dug out

the place where she had buried the coins. She got the surprise of her life to find the coins missing. She ran to the sage and said, "O sage, my coins are not at their place."

"What can I do if they are not there? You had kept them yourself. I do not know anything about them," said the sage. The woman understood that she had been cheated out of her money.

Suddenly, she remembered that Birbal was famous for his intelligence. She immediately went to Birbal for help. Birbal heard her very carefully. After thinking for some time, he said, "Don't worry. I will soon fix this problem. Do as I say." He, then, gave her some instructions.

Next day, Birbal went to the sage and said, "Great sage, I have heard a lot about your unworldliness. I am going to Agra for a few days to meet my cousin. I want to leave this bag

in your custody." Saying this, he produced a bag and opened it. It was full of jewels and pearls. The sage's eyes started shining with greed on seeing so much wealth. Just then he saw the old woman coming again. 'If she starts speaking, he will not keep the jewels with me,' he thought.

"Ah, there you are," the sage said to the old woman. "I found out in my meditation that you had kept the bag in the northern corner of the hut. Go and dig there."

The old woman went and dug up the place the sage had indicated and sure enough the coins were there. Just then, a servant of Birbal arrived. "Your cousin from Agra has come to visit you here," he said to Birbal.

"Ah, then I need not go there," Birbal said and left the place with his bag of jewels. The sage could not do anything.

THE VALUE OF SWORD

An old woman lived next to Birbal's house. One day, Birbal heard the sound of crying coming from the old woman's house. Next day, he asked the woman what the matter was. She said, "My son has passed away in a battle. Now, there is no one to look after me." Birbal took pity on the woman and asked her, "Do you have something to gift to the emperor?"

"I have nothing except an old sword that belonged to my son," replied the old woman.

"Go and gift it to the emperor. He would surely give you something in return," Birbal advised.

The old woman did as Birbal had advised. The next day, she came to the court and lifting up the sword said, "Your Majesty, my son used to work in your army. I have

brought his sword to gift it to you so that it can be used again." The emperor examined the sword and said, "Well, this sword is rusted. It cannot be used again." Then, Akbar asked a servant to give the woman some coins. Birbal knew that a few coins would not be enough for the woman. "Let me look at the sword, Your Majesty," Birbal took the sword and looked at it.

"What is the matter?" Emperor Akbar asked him.

"I have heard that a thing turns into gold when an emperor touches it. I am wondering why it hasn't happened," replied Birbal.

Akbar got the hint. He asked another servant to weigh the sword in gold coins and give them to the woman. The woman returned home happily.

One day, Emperor Akbar asked Birbal to make a list of all the blind people living in the kingdom. Birbal knew it was a difficult task as there were scores of blind people in the kingdom. After prevaricating for a while, he asked the emperor, "Your Majesty, why do you want such a list?"

"I want to give them alms, Birbal," replied the emperor.

"But, Your Majesty, the number of blind people in your kingdom is very large. In fact it is more than the number of sighted people," said Birbal to put off the matter. Akbar was very surprised to hear this. "I don't think so. If you are so sure about it then prove it to me," said Akbar.

Next day, Birbal took the frame of a cot and his servant, and went to the market. He started weaving

the cot on the roadside. He asked his servant to stand next to him with a notebook and a pen. After some time, people started coming. They would stop and stare at Birbal doing such a trivial work. "What are you doing, Birbal?" they would ask. Instead of replying, Birbal would quietly ask his servant to write down their names in his notebook. Soon people started whispering, "Birbal has gone mad. He doesn't know what he is doing. We should report the matter to the emperor."

A crowd gathered around him. Emperor Akbar too heard of Birbal's strange activity. He went out to inspect. As soon as he saw Birbal, he asked, "What are you doing, Birbal?" Birbal indicated to the servant that the emperor's name should also be written. Then, Birbal got up and said, "Your Majesty,

I have written down the names of some of the blind men of our kingdom. Have a look at this list." Saying so, Birbal handed over the list to the emperor. As the emperor started to go through the list, he was surprised to find his name also in it.

"What is this! What is my name doing in the list?" asked Akbar.

"Your Majesty, you had also asked the question, 'What are you doing?', even though it is quite plain that I am weaving a cot," replied Birbal.

The emperor started laughing at this reply. He understood that Birbal had done this to get rid of the task. "All right, since there are so many blind people, I would not ask you to make the list."

One day, Emperor Akbar was strolling in the palace with Birbal. He thought to test the intelligence of Birbal and put a question to him.

"Birbal, tell me why do we not have hair on our palms, even though we have them on our body?" Akbar asked.

Birbal was stumped for a moment. Then, he quickly replied, "You do not have any hair on your palms because you are constantly giving alms. All the hair on your palms have got rubbed off because of it."

"Ok, then tell me, why do you not have hair on your palms?" Akbar asked again.

"That is because my palms are constantly greased by taking your gifts and alms," replied Birbal.

"Birbal, it is true that no one can beat you in talks," said Akbar.

THE BRIGHTEST THING

Emperor Akbar was in mood for some discussion. He decided to ask his courtiers some questions. "Which is the brightest of all things?" he asked his courtiers. Everyone started giving different replies. Some of them said it was the milk. Others said it was cotton. One courtier insisted that it was the diamond. Birbal kept quiet. When the emperor saw that Birbal was not saying anything, he asked, "What is your opinion, Birbal?"

"I think the sunlight is the brightest of all things, Your Majesty," Birbal replied.

"Can you prove it?,"asked the emperor.

"Yes, I can," retorted Birbal.

The next day, Birbal invited Akbar to his house for an overnight stay. After dining, Akbar went to his room to sleep. When he got up in the morning, he found that all the doors and windows of the room were closed.

It was pitch dark in the room. Akbar tried to find the door to get out.

In his endeavour, he tripped over a bowl that was kept there. But he could not see what was inside. After some time, Akbar found the door.

When he opened the door, the sunlight flooded in. He turned and saw that he had tripped over a bowl full of milk. Some wads of cotton were also lying

about. Just then, Birbal came inside.

"Who had shut down all the doors and windows of my room?" asked the emperor in surprise.

"It was I, Your Majesty," replied Birbal.

"Why did you do such a senseless thing?" asked Akbar angrily.

"When it was dark, you were not able to see either the milk or cotton. You were only able to see them when sunlight came in. So which of them do you think is the brightest?" asked Birbal.

The emperor understood that Birbal had done all this to prove his point.

"I understand your point, Birbal. But next time use simpler methods," the emperor said in a relieved tone.

THE BEST WEAPON OF DEFENSE

Once, Emperor Akbar was in his armoury. He was inspecting the weapons. Actually, he wanted to know the number of weapons in his armoury. Suddenly, he asked the courtiers who were alongwith him, "What is the best weapon of defense?"

"It is the sword, Your Majesty," replied one of them. "Bows and arrows, Your Majesty," replied the second.

"What do you think Birbal?" asked the emperor.

"I think the best weapon is the one that comes immediately to hand," said Birbal. Everyone was surprised by this reply.

"What do you mean by that, Birbal?" asked the emperor.

"I can prove it to you, Your Majesty," replied Birbal.

The next day, Birbal made his preparations and took the emperor for a walk. After strolling for some time, they came to a deserted place. When they were in the middle of the lane, they suddenly saw a big dog coming towards them from the opposite direction. There was no time to run back. The dog came nearer, and was about to jump on them when Birbal picked up a stone and threw it at the dog. The dog ran back in fright. The emperor wiped his perspiration. "If you had not thrown that stone, we would have been bitten," said the emperor.

"What proved to be the best weapon, Your Majesty?" asked Birbal with a smile. "The sword or the stone?"

"Oh! Certainly, the stone," replied the emperor.

"I have proved my point," Birbal uttered boldly.

DIFFERENCE BY 16 FEET

Once, Emperor Akbar was in a jovial mood. He decided to pull Birbal's leg. He thought that it would enliven the heavy atmosphere of the court. So, he asked him, "Birbal, tell me what is the difference between you and a donkey?"

The courtiers started laughing. Birbal bowed his head down and appeared to deliberate on the question. He seemed to be calculating something while looking at the ground. "What are you calculating, Birbal?" asked the emperor.

"I was calculating the difference between me and a donkey. It appears to be about 16 feet," said Birbal.

The emperor was very embarrassed because Birbal had given the distance between him and the emperor's throne. Akbar did not mind because Birbal was his favourite courtier.

THE SHORT BLANKET

The courtiers of Akbar once gathered together and went to complain to Akbar. "Your Majesty, we are sad that you do not think us worthy of your regard in comparison to Birbal," they said in a sad voice.

"Well, it is true that I consider Birbal as the wisest among you. That is why I regard him highly," replied the emperor. "There is nothing that Birbal can do and we cannot. You should only give us a chance to prove ourselves," said the courtiers.

"Very well," said the emperor. That very day, Akbar called the courtiers to his private chamber. He was lying on his bed with a blanket covering him.

"I have a problem," said the emperor, "I am finding it difficult to cover myself fully with this blanket. Cover me up in such a manner that neither my feet

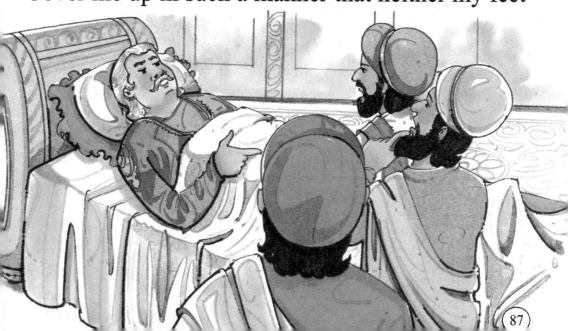

nor my head remains exposed."

The courtiers at once started trying to cover up the emperor. But the blanket was shorter than the desired length. When they covered up the feet, the head was exposed, when they covered up the head the feet were exposed. At last, they gave up trying. The emperor called a manservant and ordered him to call Birbal. When Birbal came, he posed the same problem to him. Birbal too found that the blanket was short for the emperor. He asked the emperor to fold his legs a bit. Now, the blanket covered the emperor fully. The problem was solved. After Birbal had gone away, the emperor got up and asked the courtiers, "Do you understand now why I regard Birbal so highly? Go back and do not complaint to me against him in future."

Once, Emperor Akbar was sitting with some of his courtiers when a question struck his mind. "Which is the thing that constantly moves up?" he asked.

"The sun, Your Majesty," said one of the courtiers. "No, it is the moon," said the other. "No, no," said the third. "It is the stars." The emperor was not satisfied with any of these answers.

"Birbal, what is your opinion?" asked the emperor. Birbal thought for a moment. Then, he said, "Your Majesty, all these things do move up, but they go down also. We cannot say that these things constantly move up. In my opinion there is just one thing that always moves up." "What is that?" the emperor asked with curiosity. "It is the interest of the moneylenders. No sooner have we paid back some interest, more accumulates the next month. It is constantly on our minds," Birbal replied thoughtfully.

"You are quite right, Birbal," said the emperor and rewarded him for his wise answer.

THE CRYING OF THE RIVER

Every evening, Emperor Akbar went for a stroll on the banks of the River Yamuna. Sometimes, Birbal also accompanied him. One day, Akbar and Birbal were having a walk. Akbar heard the noise of the river flowing by. He felt as if the river was crying. He asked Birbal, "Birbal, can you tell me why the river cries all the time?"

Birbal was puzzled to hear such a strange question. But he was Birbal, the great. He smiled and replied, "The river leaves his father, the mountain, and comes to see her husband, the sea. She misses her father a lot and for this reason, she always cries."

Emperor Akbar knew that he had asked Birbal a strange question. He was very impressed with Birbal's wit.

Birbal was the favourite of Emperor Akbar. It was due to his kind nature, honesty, intelligence and wit. Emperor Akbar would always think of activities to tease Birbal.

One day, an excellent idea hit him. He appointed some carpenters to make a cupboard touching which a person would get stuck to it. The carpenters spent many days and nights and thus, the cupboard was prepared. No one knew about it.

Next morning, Akbar woke up early. He placed an apple in the cupboard. Later in the day, when Birbal came to the palace, Akbar asked him to bring that apple from the cupboard. Now, Birbal was not at all aware of the emperor's intention. The cupboard was in another room.

Birbal went into the room and as soon as he was about

to open the cupboard, his hand got stuck to it. He tried a lot to free himself but to no avail. He took the support of his second hand also but it also got stuck. Birbal got tensed. He didn't want to call anyone for help as it might have lowered his  reputation as an intelligent and quick-witted man. On the other hand, when Birbal didn't return for some time, Akbar understood that he had got stuck to the cupboard. He felt very happy at his success. He quietly went to the room to see the pitiful condition of Birbal. When he reached there, he found Birbal struggling to free himself. Akbar went up to him and said, "Birbal, what happened? Did you leave your intelligence at home today?"

Birbal felt very embarrassed and didn't say anything. Akbar understood how helpless Birbal must be

feeling at that time. He somehow got him free, and asked him to go home for the day. After this event, everyday Akbar would tease Birbal by saying, "Birbal, remember the ghost of the apple?" Hearing this Birbal would feel ashamed and the emperor would enjoy.

One day, when Akbar again teased Birbal, Birbal decided to teach him a lesson. He asked for a month's leave on account of going on a pilgrimage. The emperor granted him the leave. At night, Birbal left Agra but he didn't go on pilgrimage. He went to the nearby jungle, changed his guise as a saint and returned to Agra. Then, he went to an inn and started living there. The emperor as well as the people of Agra thought that Birbal had gone to a pilgrimage. While living in the inn, Birbal kept an account of all the activities of the emperor.

One day, Emperor Akbar with some of his soldiers went to the jungle on a hunting expedition. When

Birbal came to know about the programme, he quickly went to the jungle and hid himself.

On the other hand, Akbar chased a wild boar and while doing so, he got s e p a r a t e d from his soldiers.

The wild boar ran fast and hid somewhere. The emperor decided to return back, but he could not as he was not aware of the way back to the palace and his soldiers were not with him. He was taking rest under a tree when suddenly a ghost jumped from the tree. He had long nails, pointed teeth and big hair. His red eyes frightened the emperor. He lost his sense.

When Akbar regained his senses, he found himself on his bed. Actually, his soldiers had found him in an unconscious state and brought him in the palace. The emperor felt happy that no one knew about his encounter with the ghost.

Two days after this incident, he got the news that Birbal had returned. When Birbal came to meet him, he again asked him, "How was the ghost of the apple?"

Birbal smiled and said, "Just as the ghost of the jungle." Akbar was shocked to hear this. Now he recognised the ghost he had seen in the forest. the jungle. Since that day, Akbar never teased Birbal regarding the apple.

THE LESSON IN HOSPITALITY

One day, Birbal decided to visit one of his relatives who lived in another city. He asked for permission and the emperor gave him his consent. Birbal took some food and water with him for the journey and rode towards the other town.

Now, those relatives didn't want any guest at their house. When they saw Birbal coming towards their house, they got upset. They started thinking of an idea to force Birbal to return to Agra. The husband thought of a plan. He told the idea to his wife, who also liked it. They both stood in their verandah and pretended to fight. The husband took a stick and pretended to beat his wife.

When Birbal saw this, he understood the whole matter. He decided to teach them a lesson. He quickly alighted from his horse and hid himself behind some bushes near the relative's house. On the other hand, the couple kept pretending to fight. The husband

alleged that the wife had poured too much salt in the dish. At this, the wife started shouting more loudly. After some time, they looked for Birbal. When they didn't find him, they thought that he had left. Seeing this, the husband started boasting, "See, how great my idea was! Can you ever think of such an idea?"

"You didn't praise my acting. I acted as if I was actually being beaten," said the wife.

"Yes, we are both great. Look, seeing our fight, Birbal fled from here," said the husband.

"I haven't fled," came a voice. It was Birbal. He came out of the bushes and stood in front of the couple. "I was also acting as having fled," Birbal said. The couple felt very embarrassed. They promised Birbal that henceforth they would always welcome their guests and give them a warm hospitality.

FULL MOON AND HALF MOON

Once, Emperor Akbar sent Birbal to Kabul for some important work. In Kabul, when people came across Birbal, looking at his dress, they thought that he might be a spy of some other country. When the people asked him about his identity, Birbal revealed that he was from Hindustan and had come for some important work. But the people still didn't believe him. They took him to their king.

The king of Kabul asked Birbal, "Tell me the truth. Who are you and why have you come to Kabul?"

"Your Majesty, I am Birbal. I have come for some important work. Emperor Akbar of Hindustan has sent me here," replied Birbal. "Moreover, I am very fond of travelling to different places."

"This means that you have met many kings," said the king of Kabul. "Tell me, have you ever met a king like me?"

Birbal bowed his head and said politely, "You are like the moon of full moon night."

"Then, what about your king?" asked the king of Kabul.

"He is like the half moon, Your Majesty," replied Birbal.

The king felt very pleased. He gave many gifts to Birbal and bade him goodbye. When Birbal reached Agra, he told about his meeting with the king of Kabul to everyone. When the enemies of Birbal, the jealous courtiers, came to know about it, they got a chance to poison the mind of Akbar against him. They went to Akbar and told what Birbal had said against him in the court of the king of Kabul.

Akbar understood that they were all jealous of Birbal and had come to instigate against him. But, he wanted

to see how Birbal would tackle the problem.

Next day, when Birbal reached the court, Akbar asked him about his conversation with the king of Kabul. Birbal told him everything truly. The emperor pretended to be angry and asked him, "Why did you address the king of Kabul as full moon and me as half moon?"

"Your Majesty, I only praised you. The full moon can never increase but the half moon keeps on increasing. Likewise, the king of Kabul has reached the prime point. He cannot prosper any further. But you, My Majesty, will prosper day and night."

Hearing the explanation, Akbar was much pleased. He gifted his necklace to Birbal. The jealous courtiers could not say anything.

THE COSTLY CANDLESTICKS

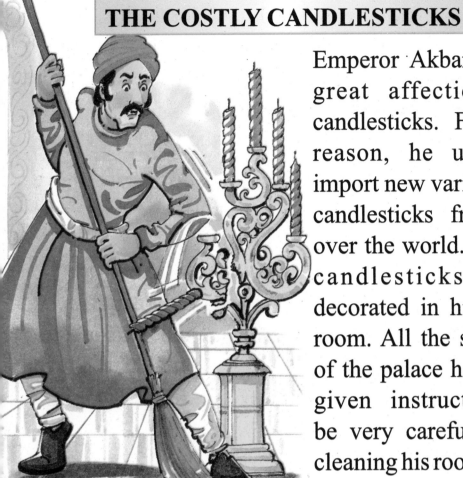

Emperor Akbar had a great affection for candlesticks. For this reason, he used to import new varieties of candlesticks from all over the world. All the candlesticks were decorated in his royal room. All the servants of the palace had been given instruction to be very careful while cleaning his room.

One day, a servant was cleaning his room, when, by mistake, a candlestick fell from his hand and broke down. He got badly scared. He started trembling with fear as to what the emperor would say to him.

When Emperor Akbar came to know about this, he got furious. He scolded the servant, "Can't you work properly? This candlestick was so costly. It was one of my favourite candlesticks."

Next day in the court, the emperor gave the servant the death sentence, and for that day, he was sent to jail. When Birbal came to know about this, he felt very upset. He had the understanding that all human beings are fallible. He went to meet the servant in the prison. He listened to the entire story of the servant. He thought of a plan and told it to the servant.

Next day, at the time of hanging, the servant was asked for his last wish. The servant wished to meet the emperor for the last time. The soldiers took the servant to the emperor. Akbar, at that time, was sitting in his royal room and was admiring his candlesticks. The servant first bowed before the emperor and then, suddenly, broke all the candlesticks. Akbar and the soldiers who had brought him there were all stunned to see this.

Akbar shouted at the servant, "Have you gone insane? How dare you break my candlesticks? That too in front of me."

The servant said with folded hands, "Your Majesty, I have just saved the lives of all those people whose lives could be in danger due to these candlesticks. I have already got the death sentence. Now, it doesn't matter whether I break one candlestick or all of them. I wished that no other servant should break your candlesticks mistakenly, or their lives will be in danger. Please understand me and forgive me."

The emperor was surprised to hear this. He realised his fault. He asked the servant, "I know you are not so intelligent to think of all this. Tell me who told you to do all this?"

"Birbal, Your Majesty," replied the servant.

Akbar looked at Birbal who had reached there by then. He thanked him saying, "Birbal, you saved me from committing a sin. You are really my well-wisher."

Birbal, one of the nine gems in the court of Emperor Akbar was world-famous. His tales of intelligence had spread far and wide. The king of Iran also heard about him. He wanted to test Birbal's intelligence. For this reason, he sent a messenger to Akbar's court and invited Birbal to Iran.

Birbal accepted the invitation and after travelling for a week, the messenger and Birbal reached Iran. The messenger took Birbal to the guesthouse that was near the palace. There, he was provided refreshments. Birbal, then, took some rest as he was feeling very tired after such a long journey.

In the evening, the messenger took Birbal to the court. As soon as he entered the court, he saw a strange scene. In the court, four identical men were sitting on four identical thrones. All the four men looked so much alike that it was very difficult for anyone to guess who was the real king. Birbal, such an intelligent person, also got confused. He had never met the king of Iran. He couldn't understand whom to greet.

He got thoughtful. Suddenly, an idea struck his mind. He didn't utter a single word and stood still. He just kept looking at all the four men minutely. The real king of Iran was waiting impatiently for Birbal to say something. After about five minutes, Birbal went to one of those men and said, "Your Majesty, greetings to you. I have come from a far off place to meet you. I have brought a message of goodwill and friendship from Emperor Akbar of Hindustan. I know that you are the real king."

The man stood up from his seat and said, "Birbal, welcome to Iran. It is my pleasure to meet you. I had heard a lot about your presence of mind and intelligence. Today, I saw it with my own eyes. You

are indeed very clever and intelligent. But tell me, how did you identify me as the real king? We never met before. Even then, you succeeded in recognising me?"

Birbal smiled and said, "Sir, I observed all four of you. The other three men were perplexed. They were thinking what to do. They looked at you quite frequently. They wanted to know how you would react, so that they could imitate you. But you, the real king had no hesitation. You kept looking straight at me."

The king of Iran was very impressed by Birbal's intelligence. He embraced Birbal and said, "You truly are the best. I admire your intelligence." Birbal stayed there for about a week. At the time of departure, the king of Iran gave many gifts to Birbal.

One day, Akbar and Birbal were roaming the streets of Agra in disguise. They were passing through a cottage when they heard shouts coming from inside.

Akbar and Birbal peeped through the window and saw that a woman was shouting at her husband. She was saying, "I gave you just one work even then you couldn't complete it. Now, go away from here and don't return till you have completed the work." The husband did not say anything. He quietly picked up a bag and left the room.

Akbar and Birbal moved ahead on their way. On returning to the palace, they discussed about the couple. Akbar asked Birbal, "Birbal, the man seemed

strong enough but still he didn't say anything to his wife. He quietly listened to what his wife was saying. Why?"

Birbal replied, "Your Majesty, this is the truth of married life. All husbands tend to listen to their wives. They cannot open their mouths in front of them."

Akbar didn't believe Birbal. He said, "Birbal, I don't think so. I listen to my wife, it's true, but not in every case."

Birbal said to the emperor, "Your Majesty, I am telling you the truth. You are the emperor. Nobody can rule you out. But, in general, every husband obeys his wife."

At this, Akbar said to Birbal, "Birbal, can you prove it to me what you are saying is correct?" Birbal agreed to prove his point to Akbar.

Next day, Birbal ordered all the married men of the kingdom to gather in front of the palace. When the men had assembled, Birbal addressed them, "All those husbands who obey their wives step to my right, and those who don't obey, step to my left."

On getting the order, all the men stepped to the right of Birbal except one. Emperor Akbar felt happy to see that he had won the argument. But, just then, Birbal asked the man, "While all the men stepped to my right, you stepped to the left. Don't you obey your wife?" "No sir, I always obey my wife. Actually, she has asked me to keep away from crowds, so, I did not step to your right."

Hearing this, Akbar, Birbal and all the men present there laughed loudly. Akbar said to Birbal, "Yes Birbal, you were right. You have proved that all husbands obey their wives."

THE MOST BEAUTIFUL

There were so many courtiers in Emperor Akbar's court who were jealous of Birbal. They always looked for the opportunity to defame Birbal.

One day, one of the courtiers went to meet Hussain Khan, Akbar's brother-in-law. He said to him, "Sir, you are queen's brother. You should hold the post which Birbal is occupying."

"Oh, it is not possible at all," said Hussain Khan, "Birbal is very intelligent. The emperor will never accept me as his advisor. Moreover, I am not so witty as Birbal." "Just ask your sister, the queen, to recommend your name. The emperor can never turn down the request made by the queen," said the courtier.

Hussain Khan agreed. He went to meet his sister and told her about his feelings. That night, when Emperor Akbar went to his room, he saw queen in a displeased mood. He asked her the reason, to which the queen replied, "I want my brother, Hussain Khan to get the post that Birbal holds. He is appropriate for that."

At this, Emperor Akbar said, "I can't make Hussain Khan my advisor. He is not worth it. He is not so witty and intelligent as Birbal. Moreover, he is foolish and stubborn. Furthermore, I don't have any strong reason to replace Birbal."

The queen thought of a plan. She said to the emperor, "Tomorrow evening, ask Birbal to fetch me to go for a walk with you in the royal garden. I will refuse and when he won't be able to persuade me, you can dismiss him." At first, Emperor Akbar didn't agree as Birbal was not only his advisor but his friend also, but when the queen requested repeatedly, he agreed. Next evening, when Emperor Akbar and Birbal were in the garden, Akbar said to Birbal, "Birbal, the queen is angry with me. Please go and persuade her to come for a walk with me. If you fail to fulfil my wish, I will dismiss you and give your post to Hussain Khan."

Birbal understood that it was a plan of the queen to remove him from his post. He made a plan with a servant and went to the chamber of the queen. He had only said these words, "Your Majesty, the emperor

wants you to join him for a ..." when the same servant came and said something to Birbal.

The only thing the queen could hear was "The most beautiful.." Then, Birbal turned to the queen and said that the plan had changed and walked away from there. The queen became thoughtful. She thought that the emperor must have found some beautiful woman for company. She rushed to the garden where Akbar was strolling. Akbar was surprised to see the queen there. He asked her why she had come to the garden. The queen till now had understood that she had been befooled by Birbal. She told everything to the emperor and accepted that Hussain Khan could not replace intelligent Birbal.